A Giant First-Start Reader

This easy reader contains only 42 different words, repeated often to help the young reader develop word recognition and interest in reading.

Basic word list for *Trouble in Space*

a	glad	oh
and	go	on
back	goes	quick
be	going	ready
blast	gone	space
blasting	he	Teddy
comes	here	that
coming	in	there
down	into	this
Earth	is	through
fast	leaving	to
faster	no	trip
for	not	trouble
getting	off	try

Trouble in Space

Written by Rose Greydanus

Illustrated by Don Page

Troll Associates

Library of Congress Cataloging in Publication Data

Greydanus, Rose.
    Trouble in space.

    Summary: Teddy is glad to take a trip into
space until he runs into trouble.
    [1. Space flight—Fiction. 2. Science fiction]
I. Page, Don. II. Title.
PZ7.G876Tr   [E]   81-5114
ISBN 0-89375-517-6 (case)   AACR2
ISBN 0-89375-518-4 (pbk.)

Here comes Teddy.

Teddy is going on a trip.

Teddy is going into space.

He is getting ready.

Teddy is ready for a space trip.

Teddy is ready for blast off.

Blast off!

There he goes.

Teddy is going . . . going . . . gone!

Teddy is leaving Earth.

He is blasting through space.

He is glad to be in space.

Go, Teddy, go!

Teddy is going fast.

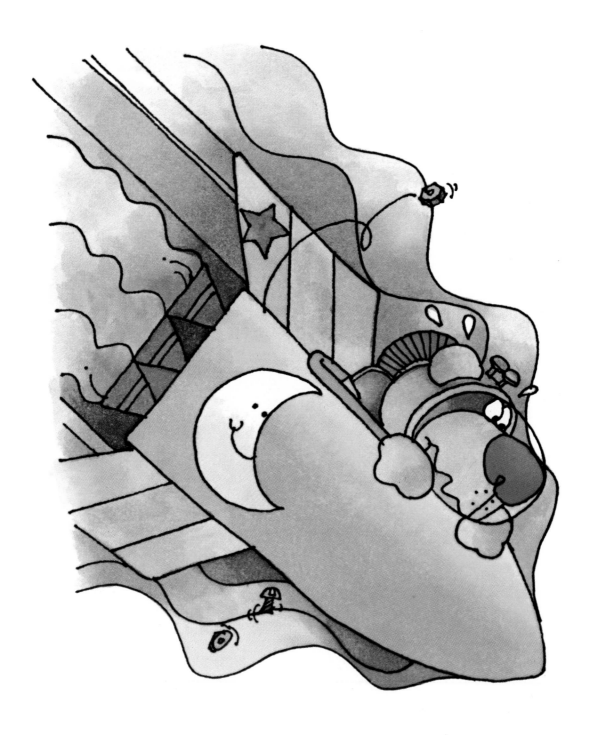

He is going faster and faster.

Oh no! Here comes trouble.

Teddy is in trouble.

There is trouble in space.

Teddy is not glad to be in space.

Quick, Teddy, try this.

Oh no! Try that, Teddy!

Teddy is leaving space.

He is coming back to Earth.

Teddy is coming down . . . down . . . down.

Here comes Teddy.

He is glad to be back.

Teddy is glad to be back on Earth!